Anonymous

A Christian Family Service Book

Anonymous

A Christian Family Service Book

Reprint of the original, first published in 1859.

1st Edition 2022 | ISBN: 978-3-37512-084-9

Verlag (Publisher): Salzwasser Verlag GmbH, Zeilweg 44, 60439 Frankfurt, Deutschland
Vertretungsberechtigt (Authorized to represent): E. Roepke, Zeilweg 44, 60439 Frankfurt, Deutschland
Druck (Print): Books on Demand GmbH, In de Tarpen 42, 22848 Norderstedt, Deutschland

A CHRISTIAN

𝕱𝔞𝔪𝔦𝔩𝔶 𝔖𝔢𝔯𝔳𝔦𝔠𝔢 𝔅𝔬𝔬𝔨

OR

DAILY PRAYER AND DAILY PRAISE.

TO WHICH IS PREFIXED A

LIST OF SELECTED LESSONS

FROM THE HISTORICAL AND PROPHETICAL BOOKS OF THE

OLD TESTAMENT.

FOR FAMILY USE THROUGHOUT THE YEAR.

———◆———

BY A CLERGYMAN OF THE CHURCH OF ENGLAND.

———◆———

"Choose you this day whom ye will serve—as for me and my house we will serve the Lord."—Josh. xxiv. 15.

———

BICESTER:

PRINTED BY E. SMITH AND SON,

1859.

The Lord's Prayer.

OUR Father which art in heaven, Hallowed be thy name; Thy kingdom come; Thy will be done in earth, as it is in heaven: Give us this day our daily bread; And forgive us our trespasses, as we forgive them that trespass against us; And lead us not into temptation, But deliver us from evil; For thine is the kingdom, the power, and the glory, for ever and ever. Amen.

The Apostolical Benediction.
2 Cor. xiii. 14.

THE Grace of our Lord Jesus Christ, and the love of God, and the fellowship of the Holy Ghost, be with us all evermore. Amen.

Or,

The Aaronic Benediction.
Numb. vi. 24—26.

THE Lord bless us and keep us. The Lord make His face to shine upon us. The Lord lift up the light of His countenance upon us, and give us peace now and for evermore. Amen.

PREFACE.

THE writer's object, in the following pages, is to offer to heads of families such forms of Prayer and Praise as may habituate a Christian household to the doctrines and duties of our holy religion. The knowledge of these is often imperfectly gathered from the public services of the Church; nor will occasional catechetical teaching (even had all persons the benefit of it) produce the effectual impression on the mind resulting from the daily use of words which (it is hoped,) truly, and plainly, though in varied language, express the feelings an intelligent christian ought to entertain. Much will be gained if we can learn habitually to pray and praise God according to the full practical *Faith* of a christian, and the guidance of the Holy Spirit. The writer has endeavoured to excite and fix a thoughtful attention, during the reading of these family services, by avoiding generalities, and by following as closely as possible the language, as well as the guidance of scripture. The Prayers are also broken into the form of collects, that they may admit of being differently combined, and of forming longer or shorter services, as occasion may require. The table of "Selected Lessons" is introduced in order to remove a difficulty in the way of reading the Old Testament aloud. It is of the *Old Testament* scriptures that St. Paul says they "are able to make thee wise unto salvation through faith which is in Christ Jesus." And it is scarcely too much to say that without a familiar knowledge of the Old Testament, the New *cannot be thoroughly appreciated or understood.*

In the selection now offered, as much as possible has been included consistently with the purpose of bringing the whole into 365 lessons of moderate length, one for each day throughout the year.

CONTENTS.

Selected Lessons.

OBSERVE.—Occasionally it will be enough to omit or paraphrase a clause *in* a verse: elsewhere the verse itself must be omitted or paraphrased. Direction will be given accordingly.

The chapters appointed in the *Book of Common Prayer* to be read on Sundays and the Great Festivals, are not included in the following list.

Genesis
4
7
8
13
14
15
16 & 17 v 1—10
20 omit v 18
21
23
24 v 1—31
24 v 32—67
28
31 v 1—9 & 14—34
31 v 36—55
32
33
37
40
41 v 1—36
41 v 37—57
44
47
48

Genesis
49
50
Exodus
1 (omit 15—21)
    and c 2
4 omit v 24—26
7
8
15
16
17
18
19 omit in v 15
20
21 omit v 22—25
22 omit v 16 17 & 19
23
24
25
26
27
28 v 1—41
30 v 11—16 & c 31
32

Exodus
33
34 paraph. v 16 &
    19
40
Leviticus
1 & 2 v 1—11
2 v 12—16 & c 3
5
9 v 22—24 & c 10
14 v 1—32
16
19 omit v 19—22
    and 29
23
24
25 v 1—34
25 v 35—55
26 v 1—26
26 v 27—46
Numbers
1 v 1—4 & c 2
6
9
10

Numbers	Joshua	1 Samuel
11	7	8
12	8	9
13	9	10
14 omit in v 33	11	11
15 omit in v 39	24	14 v 1—23
17 & 18 v 1—7	Judges	14 v 24—52
20	1	16
21	2 omit in v 17	18 omit in v 25—27
27	3 paraph. v 21	19
32	omit 22	20
33 v 1—33	6	21 omit in v 4 &
35	7	v 5
Deuteronomy	8 paraph. in v 27	22
1	and 33	23
2	9 v 1—29	24
3	9 v 30—57	25 v 1—21
11	10	25 v 23—44 omit
15	11 v 1—33	v 34
17	11 v 34—40 & c 12	26
18	13	27 and 29
20	14	28
21 (omit in v 13)	15	30 v 1—26
& c 22 v 1—5	16 omit v 1	31
24 v 10—22 & c	17 & 18 v 1—6	2 Samuel
25 v 1—4	18 v 7—31	1
26	20 v 1—25	2
28 v 1—29	20 v 26—48	3 v 12—39 omit
28 v 31—68	21 omit v 11 and	in v 14
29	in v 12	4 and 5
30	Ruth	6
31	1 omit in v 11 &	7
32 v 1—44	v 12, 13	8 and 9
33	2	10 omit in v 4
34	3	15
Joshua	4	16 v 1—19
1	1 Samuel	17 omit v 25
2	1	18
3.	4	20 omit v 3
4	5 omit in v 9	23 v 1—23
5	6	1 Kings
6	7	1 v 5—40

1 Kings	1 Chronicles	Ezra
1 v 41—53 & c	17	4
2 v 1—11	21	5
2 v 12—46	22	6
3	28	7
4 v 29—34 & c. 5	29	8 v 15—36
6	2 Chronicles	9
8 v 1—40	1	10 v 1—17
8 v 41—66	2	Nehemiah
9	3 and 4	1
10	5	2
11	6	3
12	7	4
14 paraph. in v 10	8 omit, except in	5
omit v 24	Leap year	6 & 7 v 1—4
15 omit in v 12	9	8
16 omit in v 11	10 & 11 v 1—17	9
20	12	10 v 28—39
2 Kings	13	12 v 27—47
1	14	13
2	15	Esther
3	16	1
4	18	2
6	19 & 20 v 1—13	3
7	20 v 14—37	4
8 omit in v 12	21 paraph. in v 13	5
12	22 & 23	6
13	24	7
14	25	8
15	26 & 27	9 and 10
16	28	Isaiah
17	29	3 (omit v 17) & 4
20	30	6 and 7
21	31	8 and 9
22	32	10
23 v 36 37 & c 24	33	13
25	34	14
1 Chronicles	35	28
10 & 11 v 1—25	36	29
12 v 16—40	Ezra	34 and 35
13 and 14	1 & 2 v 1 & 64—70	40
15 v 1—3 & c 16	3	42

Isaiah	Ezekiel	Obadiah
45	21	Jonah
48	27	1 and 2
49	33	3 and 4
52	34	Micah
54	36	4 and 5
60	37	7
61 and 62	38 & 39 v 21—29	Nahum
63	47	1 and 2
Jeremiah	Daniel	Habakkuk
4 omit in v 4	1	1
7	2	Zephaniah
11	4	3
17	5	Haggai
28	9	1
29	12	2
31	Hosea	Zechariah
33	10 and 11	1 and 2
34	13 (omit in v 16)	3 and 4
38 v 1—10 & c 39	and c 14	5 and 6
42	Joel	7 and 8
44	1	9 and 10
52	3	11
Ezekiel	Amos	12 and 13
1	1 (paraph. in v 13)	14
3	& 2 omit in v 7	Malachi
8 and 9	3 and 4	1 and 2
10	5	3 and 4
11	6 and 7	
12	8 and 9	

N.B. The New Testament may be read throughout, excepting perhaps the 8th chapter of St. John, where omit 1—11.

Family Prayers,

&c.

---◆---

General Thanksgiving for Morning Prayer.

"Rather rejoice because your names are written in heaven."—Luke x. 20.

WE praise and thank Thee, Almighty and merciful God, for that Thou hast spared us through the night past; that Thou hast preserved us from all dangers, and brought us safe to the beginning of another day. We bless Thee for our creation, and that Thou hast enabled us to enjoy much happiness in this life; but chiefly would we rejoice in this, because Thou hast given us hope of exceeding blessedness in the life to come. Lord, in Thy mercy bring us to that eternal life through Jesus Christ. Suffer us not to lose it, or to be disappointed of our hope. Leave us not, nor forsake us, neither let us forsake Thee: but direct sanctify and govern us in all our doings. Chasten, humble, and purify our hearts by fatherly correction, and the inspiration of Thy Holy Spirit; that, this life having been spent in Thy service, we may pass through death to a joyful Resurrection unto everlasting felicity, through Jesus Christ our Lord.   Amen.

Or this.

"Bless the Lord, O my soul; and forget not all his benefits."—Ps. ciii. 2.

WE thank and praise and glorify Thee, O Lord God of our salvation, for all Thy mercies towards us.   Thou hast not dealt with us after our deservings, but according to the abundance of Thy loving-kindness.   Hitherto hast Thou brought us and spared us.   Spare us, O heavenly Father, and be with us still; that we may live this day and ever, to Thy glory; and serve Thee faithfully to our own great comfort, through Jesus Christ our Lord.   Amen.

———

One of the following to be used at Evening Prayer.

"Thou shalt not be afraid for the terror by night, nor for the arrow that flieth by day, for the pestilence that walketh in darkness, nor for the destruction that wasteth at noonday."—Ps. xci. 5, 6.

O GOD, with whom the darkness is no darkness, but the night is as clear as the day.   The darkness and the light to Thee are both alike; Hear us, we beseech Thee, and watch over us this night, and let no evil come near our dwelling. We thank and praise Thee for Thy mercies to us this day: for our preservation in the midst of unseen dangers, and for the many blessings Thou hast given us to enjoy. Specially we praise Thee for the light of Thy gospel—for the means of grace, and for the hope of glory. Accept for Thy dear Son's sake whatever we have done with the desire to please Thee. Forgive also for His sake whatever we have done amiss in negligence, or ignorance, or wilful sin. Cleanse and amend our hearts by the inspiration of Thy Holy Spirit. Quicken our zeal to serve Thee. Confirm our faith in the salvation of Thy Son. Renew and increase in us Thy grace. So teach us to number our days that we may apply our hearts unto wisdom; and diligently prepare ourselves for Thy judgment, before the night cometh when no man can work. Grant this, O heavenly Father, for Jesus Christ's sake, our Lord. Amen.

Or this.

"The Lord will command his loving-kindness in the day-time, and in the night his song shall be with me, and my prayer unto the God of my life:—Ps. xlii. 8.

FOR all Thy mercies, O God, this day, we praise and thank Thee, and magnify Thy holy name. Glory be to Thee in the highest, and on earth peace, goodwill towards men. Let Thy goodwill be continued to us. Defend us this night from all dangers; and give us ever the desire to love, and serve, and please Thee, through Jesus Christ our Saviour. Amen.

OCCASIONAL PRAYERS.

To be used during Ember weeks.

"They watch for your souls, as they that must give account."—Heb. xiii. 17.

LORD Jesus, who hast committed Thy Church on earth to the care of Ministers and Pastors, that they may feed Thy flock with saving knowledge, and wholesome instruction from the scripture of Truth; we beseech Thee both to guide with Thy spirit those who ordain men to this ministry, and upon all who are ordained to pour Thine abundant grace, that they may faithfully, diligently and effectually preach the gospel of Thy salvation; and by the mighty working of Thy Spirit may win many souls from Satan unto God, through Thee our only Lord and Saviour. Amen.

For Christmas.

"Comfort ye, comfort ye my people, saith your God." Is. xl. 1.

O HEAVENLY Father who as at this time didst send Thy Son into the world to be clothed in all

the infirmities of our nature, that we might have
a merciful High Priest, and a Judge who could
have compassion on us "because He is a Son
of Man;" give us grace to rejoice before Thee
with a holy joy for this Thine unspeakable mercy,
and evermore to cleave unto our Saviour with all
thankfulness and loving obedience to His words,
through the same Thy Son Jesus Christ our
Lord. Amen.

For Ash Wednesday and Lent.

"They seek me daily, and delight to know my ways, as a
nation that did righteousness, and forsook not the ordi-
nance of their God."—Is. lviii. 2.

O LORD God of truth who canst neither deceive,
nor be deceived, make us to know, as Thou
knowest, the corruptions of our hearts. Take
from us all hypocrisy. Make our repentance and
humiliation sincere. If need be, chasten and
correct us in Thy fatherly love, that we fail not
in our duty to Thee, nor lose Thy precious gift of
salvation unto eternal life, through Jesus Christ
Thy Son our Lord. Amen.

For Good Friday.

"Though your sins be as scarlet, they shall be as white as
snow."—Is. i. 18.

O JESUS, our Saviour, who from Thy cross
didst promise unto the Penitent, "To day shalt

thou be with Me in Paradise;" let our penitence
bring us also thither through Thy mighty power to
save. Lord, remember us now that Thou art come
into Thy kingdom. Incline our hearts to acknow-
ledge Thee even in the hour and in the agony of
death; and (long before) prepare us for that hour
by repentance and faith in Thee our only Saviour
and Redeemer. Amen.

For Easter.

"It is the spirit that quickeneth."—John vi. 63.

BLESSED Lord, who hast received of Thy Father
to have life in Thyself, and to quicken whom Thou
wilt, we beseech Thee, quicken us unto everlasting
life. Raise us up at the last day by the eternal
Spirit, as Thou raisedst Thine own body from the
grave. And so long as we abide on earth enable
us to keep our Passover with the unleavened bread
of sincerity and truth, rejoicing before Thee in
holiness, and in the blessed hope of a resurrection
to eternal life through Thee our Redeemer and
our God. Amen.

For Ascension Day.

"This same Jesus which is taken up from you into heaven, shall so come in like manner as ye have seen him
go into heaven."—Acts i. 11.

BLESSED Jesus Immanuel, now Man with God,
as once Thou wast God with us. Look down with
mercy on Thy Church. Watch over us. Keep us

in Thy truth. Defend us from all dangers. Make our peace with Thy Father. Lift up our hearts to Thee. And in Thine own appointed time come again to us, and receive us to Thyself, our loving Master and Saviour, no less than our Lord and our God. Amen.

For Whit-Sunday.

"I will not leave you comfortless: I will come to you.—John xiv. 18.

COMFORT us, O blessed Jesus, by the Holy Ghost, whom the Father, as on this day, sent unto His elect in Thy name. Let Thy grace be shed abundantly upon us, and on all Thy whole Church. Stir up Thy gifts in us that we may bring forth fruits of holiness, Renew in us Thy spirit; and make us perfect in every good work to do Thy will; working in us that which is pleasing in Thy sight, our only Mediator and Redeemer. Amen.

PRAYERS
FOR EACH MORNING AND EVENING THROUGHOUT THE WEEK.
Sunday Morning.

"Humble yourselves in the sight of the Lord, and He shall lift you up."—James iv. 10.

O HOLY and Heavenly Father, Thou that dwellest in the "high and holy place," but "with him

also that is of a contrite and humble spirit," who
wilt not "contend for ever, neither be always
wrath," for our "spirit should fail before Thee,"
and "the souls which Thou hast made:" Thou
hast seen our ways, yet heal us; lead us also, and
restore comforts unto us, and to all that mourn
before Thee; say unto us "Peace, peace, and I will
heal you."   "Behold, the Lord's hand is not
shortened that it cannot save, neither His ear
heavy that it cannot hear." Our "iniquities have
separated between us and our God; our sins have
hid His face from us."   Yet, O God, our Father,
let Thine arm bring salvation to us, and let Thy
spirit be upon us.   Turn us from our transgressions, and forgive us; and blot out the remembrance of our sins, for Thy dear Son's sake Jesus
Christ our Lord.   Amen.

"If we suffer, we shall also reign with him."—2 Tim.
ii. 12.

O LORD our Mediator and Redeemer; Jesus, Son
of God, and Son of man; who, as on this day of the
week, didst rise from the dead, and "become the
first fruits of them that sleep," give us grace, that
we, being dead unto sin, may in this life rise again
and live unto righteousness.   Mortify in us all
sinful desires, all worldly affections, all pride of
heart, and whatever in us is opposed to Thy Holy

Spirit. Make us to die with Thee here, that we may live Thee hereafter. Make us to suffer with Thee on earth, that we may reign with Thee when Thou comest to raise our bodies from the grave. Grant that with obedient hearts we may hear and receive Thy holy word. Grant that we may have the will and the courage to follow Thee in all holiness and pureness of living. Grant us also faith in Thee our Saviour, that we may trust not to our own righteousness, but to the great Sacrifice which Thou the Lamb of God, hast offered for us upon the cross; and to that everlasting covenant, which was ratified in Thy most precious blood: that so seeking before all things the kingdom of God and His righteousness, we may find all things needful for us in this life, and may be brought through Thee to life eternal, to dwell with Thee, our Lord and King, for ever and ever. Amen.

"As many as are led by the Spirit of God, they are the sons of God."—Rom. viii. 14.

O HOLY Spirit, Lord and giver of life, that sanctifiest all whom our Heavenly Father chooseth; sanctify us this day and evermore; that we whom He hath called, may be chosen also, among the elect people of God. Give us the heart to pray earnestly for Thy presence in us—for Thy guidance, Thy help, and comfort—that blessed gift, and those "good things" which our Father will surely give to them that ask Him. And do Thou evermore dwell within us to be our strength and counsellor, "to guide our feet into the way of peace," to quicken us unto everlasting life. Thou governest, and sanctifiest, the whole body of the Church; give faith and holiness, truth and sincerity, peace and harmony among us all. And make us—the living stones of the spiritual temple of our Lord—to live together in godly love, as sheep of one fold, as servants of one Master, and above all, as children of one Father, through Jesus Christ our Saviour and Redeemer. Amen.

[Here, as after each morning service, may be added the longer or shorter Thanksgiving, *to conclude with the* Lord's Prayer *and the* Grace.]—*See page 9.*

Sunday Evening.

"That all men should honour the Son, even as they honour the Father.—John v. 23.

O LAMB of God, who wast slain, and art alive for evermore, and hast redeemed us to God by Thy Blood; and hast made us unto our God kings and priests; Thou art worthy, O Lord, to receive blessing, and honour, and glory, and power, for Thou hast created all things, and for Thy pleasure they are, and were created. We thank Thee, O

God, for all Thy mercies towards us; but specially
we thank and praise Thee for that Thou hast
sanctified one day in seven to Thy service—to
our bodily rest, and spiritual refreshment. Let
the prayers be heard which we and all Thy faithful servants have offered unto Thee, and through
Thee this day. Forgive our sins; accept our
sacrifice of Praise and Thanksgiving; as also of
a penitent, a broken and contrite heart. Pardon
the imperfection of all our devotions. Thou, who
knowest the weakness of our mortal nature, and
the temptation of worldly cares to draw off our
thoughts from Thee and heavenly things, strength-
en us by Thy Holy Spirit day by day; Enable us
to resist the power of temptation, and to grow in
grace, and in obedience to Thy will; that so we
may be brought to the everlasting Rest which
Thou hast promised to Thy saints; and there may
live with Thee, and praise and worship Thee our
Saviour and Redeemer, who livest and reignest
with the Father, and the Holy Spirit, one God,
for ever and ever. Amen.

"Beloved, if God so loved us, we ought also to love one
another."—1 John iv. 11.

ALMIGHTY Father, who hast manifested Thy
great love for us in sending into the world Thine
only begotten Son, that we might live through

Him; send, we beseech Thee, Thy Holy Spirit
into our hearts, that we may become like unto
Him who, while we were yet sinners, died for us.
Mortify in us every thought that proceedeth from
hatred and ill will.   Let that spirit dwell in us
that dwelt in Him who, when He was reviled,
. reviled not again; when He suffered, He threat-
ened not.   Give us grace to love one another as
He hath loved us.   Fill our hearts with such perfect love and charity one towards another, that
we may be known of all men to be His Disciples,
children of one Father through Him—even of
Thee our Creator who lovest us with a father's
love, for Jesus Christ's sake our only Mediator
and Redeemer.   Amen.

———

"Baptising them in the name of the Father, and of the
  Son, and of the Holy Ghost."—Mat. xxviii. 19.

WE praise Thee, we bless Thee, we glorify Thee,
O Holy Blessed and Glorious Trinity.   We ac-
knowledge the mercies we have received from
Father, Son, and Holy Ghost.

O Holy Spirit, Lord and giver of life, we beseech Thee, sanctify us wholly.   Dwell with us.
Guide our steps.   Enlighten our understandings.
Purify our hearts.   Make us to show forth before
all men that Thou dwellest in us, by pureness, by
knowledge, by good report, by gentleness, meek-

ness, and charity; and mightily quicken us unto
everlasting life through Jesus Christ our Lord.
Amen.

[*Here, as at the end of each Evening Service, may follow
the longer or shorter General Evening Prayer, after which
the Lord's Prayer, and the Grace.*]—*See page* 10.

Monday Morning.

"Ye have not received the spirit of bondage again to fear,
but ye have received the spirit of adoption, whereby we
cry, Abba, Father".—Rom. viii. 15.

O HEAVENLY Father, who hast adopted us to
be Thy children through Jesus Christ Thy Son;
and givest the spirit of adoption to them that are
Thine, that they may love Thee as dear children,
and live according to Thy will: we beseech Thee
to hear us, and to shed abroad this spirit in our
hearts. Thou hast called us to Thy salvation, and
received us into the kingdom of Thy Son: give
us grace to walk worthy of our calling. Make us
ever mindful that we are *Christians*—that we have
been washed and sanctified from the corruption of
the world—that Thou hast in mercy put away
our sins for Thy holy covenant's sake, and by the
precious blood of Thy dear Son. Grant us the
earnest care, as well as the strength of purpose to
resist temptation that we may continue to be clean.
Make us jealously to guard the treasure of our
salvation, that we lose it not again. Enable us

to show ourselves that we are not of this world, even as the holy kingdom, to which we belong, is not of this world. And by the practice of every christian virtue make us to magnify Thee, and to advance the glory of Thy name, through Jesus Christ our Lord. Amen.

"Your heavenly Father knoweth that ye have need of all these things."—Mat. vi. 32.

O GOD who knowest that we have need of many things, and hast filled the earth with Thy riches for our sustenance and comfort: grant that while we labour to supply our bodily wants, (while we seek pleasures for our refreshment and even luxuries for our greater comfort in this life); yet we may never forget Thee. Thou that art the giver of all these blessings, accept our thanks and praise. Make us to remember those who are less amply supplied with blessings than ourselves. Make us to think of those who lack food while we have abundance—who, while we have our comforts, have not where to lay their heads. But above all worldly riches, joys, or comforts, make us seek and value, and do Thou in mercy grant, the heavenly riches of Thine abundant grace. Teach us to labour, not for the meat which perisheth, but for that which endureth unto eternity; not for the bread of this world, but for the bread

which cometh down from heaven, even Thy dear
Son the Bread of Life. Nourish our souls with
this; and refresh us with the waters of salvation,
the ever springing well of Thy Holy Spirit,
through Jesus Christ our Lord. Amen.

Monday Evening.

"Our light affliction which is but for a moment, worketh
for us a far more exceeding and eternal weight of
glory."—2 Cor. iv. 17.

O GOD, in whose hands are the issues of life and
death; who blessest, and chastenest—yea, and
makest thy bitterest chastisements to become
blessings: Hear us we beseech Thee, and so incline our hearts to love Thee, that all things may
work together for our good. We thank and praise
Thee for Thy mercies to us this day; believing
all things that befall us to be mercies from Thine,
our heavenly Father's, hand. Teach us to believe this more and more. Teach us to measure
Thy goodness towards us, not by the rule of
worldly blessings; not by the amount of riches,
or enjoyments, or. bodily comforts, which Thou
givest us in this world, but by Thy care to bring
us through things temporal to the life and the
blessedness which are eternal. Make us, O God,
to set our affections on things above, not on things
on the earth. Help us to lay up our treasure

there, where none can rob us of it, or destroy it.
And give us grace to have our conversation in
heaven, as true citizens of the heavenly kingdom
of Thy Son Jesus Christ, through whom alone we
lift up unto Thee these our Prayers. Amen.

"A man's life consisteth not in the abundance of the
things which he possesseth."—Luke xii. 15.

O JESUS our only Saviour, who hast warned us
against covetousness; against the deceitfulness of
riches; and the being engrossed by worldly cares:
so guide us, we beseech Thee, with Thy Holy
Spirit, that while we labour to do our duty in the
station of life where Thou hast placed us, we may
yet avoid those dangers; and live unto Thee as
faithful servants, and loving disciples; taking up
our cross daily for thy sake, our only Mediator
and Redeemer. Amen.

"The Lord thy God walketh in the midst of thy camp to
deliver thee and to give up thine enemies before thee.
Therefore shall thy camp be holy, that He see no un-
clean thing in thee, and turn away from thee."—Deut.
xxiii. 14.

O LORD God, who walkest in the midst of the
camp of thy saints, to deliver them, and to give
up their enemies before them, and hast said
"Therefore shall thy camp be holy," put away
from us all uncleanness; and whatsoever in us
may offend Thine eyes. Make us to feel that

Thou art among us—that Thou art close at hand to watch, and to record against us all that we do amiss. Give us grace to cleanse and purify our hearts that we may rejoice in Thy presence, and take comfort in the thought that Thou our mighty Deliverer art ever about our paths and beds. Defend us, O Lord our God, from all dangers to our bodies, and to our souls. Give up our spiritual enemies before us, even the sinful affections and deceitfulness of our own hearts. Enable us to overcome these, and to subdue them utterly, and to walk before Thee in all holiness and pureness of living, through Jesus Christ our Lord. Amen.

Tuesday Morning.

"Now all these things happened unto them for ensamples, and they are written for our admonition."—1 Cor. x. 11.

ALMIGHTY God, who has caused Thy holy scriptures to be written for our learning, and Thy dealings with men of old time to be recorded for our ensample and admonition, grant unto us abundantly the light of Thy Holy Spirit, that we may not only read, and learn, but diligently lay to heart the lessons Thou wouldest teach us—meekly receiving them, and understanding them aright. Let those holy scriptures make us wise unto salvation by Thine unerring guidance to our minds. Let no fond conceit of ours lead us rather to cherish "a private interpretation," than submit ourselves to Thy general declarations of what is true and profitable for us to know. But let us so read Thy messages of mercy, that we feel the more the terrors of Thy wrath; and so let us perceive the justice of Thy wrath, that we may be more sensible of the greatness of Thy mercy. Grant us also that by patience and comfort of the scriptures we may have hope—even the blessed hope of everlasting life, through Jesus Christ our Lord. Amen.

"Watch ye; stand fast in the faith; quit you like men; be strong."—1 Cor. xvi. 13.

O LORD Jesus Christ, who for our sake didst submit to be tempted, and in the weakness of our nature to feel the power of our subtle adversary's assaults. Look down upon us, we beseech Thee, and by the spirit which was then in Thee give us strength to resist, as Thou resistedst, every temptation of the Devil, the world, and the flesh. Defend us, O Lord, with the shield of Faith in Thee. And clothe us with the whole armour of God, that we may be able to withstand in the evil day. Impart unto us the spirit of truth, of faith, and of righteousness. And in all our temptations give us courage to fight, as in Thy sight, valiantly; believing that, "they that be with us are more

than they that be with them,"—that Thou who
art with us art mightier than He which is against
us. Thou who knowest our weakness, preserve
us from the presumptuous thought that we may
thrust ourselves into danger safely. Rather *lead
us not into temptation*, lest we resist, not sin, but
the warnings of Thy Holy Spirit. Help us con-
tinually so to watch and pray that we sin not;
but may overcome the Evil One through Thee;
and that our names be not blotted out from the
Book of Life. Hear us, O merciful Jesus, our
strength and our Redeemer. Amen.

Tuesday Evening.

" Seest thou these great buildings ? There shall not be
left one stone upon another that shall not be thrown
down."—Mark xiii. 2. See Is. lxvi. 1, 2.

O GOD, who from the beginning hast prepared
the kingdom of Thy Son Jesus Christ, moving the
Prophets by Thy Holy Spirit, and by them speak-
ing unto our fathers, that He, our Lord and
Saviour might be manifested in due time, grant
that we may in such wise read, and understand
the teaching of Thy Holy Spirit, that we may be
ready both in body and mind to obey the calling
of our heavenly King. Help us to see in Him
the way of everlasting life; to trust in Him as
the great, and only atoning sacrifice for our sins—
as our only Mediator and Intercessor with Thee,

Let no blindness or perversion of heart hide from us the true nature of His kingdom. Make us to see in it that exceeding glory which truly belongs to spiritual and heavenly things: that we seek not to glorify Thee by worldly show, and the outward magnificence which pleaseth the eye of man; but by cultivating thine own gifts of a meek and loving spirit; purifying ourselves from the corruption of the flesh, and in all holy joy and quietness shewing forth the fruits of Thy Spirit, through Jesus Christ our Lord. Amen.

"The Lord sware, and will not repent, Thou art a Priest for ever after the order of Melchesidec."—Heb. vii. 21.

THOU, O Christ, who camest to do Thy Father's will for our sanctification—Thou art our Great High Priest, having received that unchangeable Priesthood which passeth not from one to another. Thou alone art our Priest, as Thou alone art our sacrifice for sin. O Lamb of God, who Thyself barest our sins in Thine own Body on the tree, hear us, O Lord, we beseech Thee, and give us faith in Thee; that we may believe Thee to be our Saviour and Redeemer—our Lord and Master—our Resurrection and our Life. We know that by Thine Almighty power and never failing providence Thou rulest and providest for our life and well being in this world. Enable us to feel that Thou hast also died for us, and offered Thyself a sacrifice to save us unto life eternal. Make us thankful therefore as for unspeakable blessings vouchsafed to us for our welfare, both here and hereafter, through Thy great mercy and loving-kindness, O Jesus our Lord and our God. Amen.

Wednesday Morning.

"I said I will confess my transgressions unto the Lord : and thou forgavest the iniquity of my sin."—Ps. xxxii. 5.

O GOD our heavenly Father, who art of purer eyes than to behold evil, and canst not look upon iniquity, that wilt by no means clear the guilty, and yet forgivest transgression and sin for Thy dear Son's sake : O Lord God, merciful and gracious, long suffering and abundant in goodness and truth, keeping mercy for thousands of them that love Thee; we confess our manifold transgressions by thought, word, and deed, against Thy holy laws. We have left undone those things which we ought to have done, and we have done those things which we ought not to have done, and there is no health us. We have many times forgotten Thee; we have neglected Thy service; we have mis-used Thy blessings; we have made Thy mercies to us an occasion to provoke Thee, by unthankfully employing them in the indulgence of our own carnal will. Yet, O gracious Lord, who hast proclaimed Thyself "a Merciful God," have mercy upon us. Enter not into judgment with us. Be not extreme to mark what we have done amiss. Impute not perverseness unto Thy servants; but have compassion on our infirmities. Forgive our sins, and by the abundant grace of Thy Holy Spirit strengthen us that we resist temptation, and sin no more. Comfort us, O heavenly Father, by faith in Thy promises of mercy through Chirst—by the assurance that for His sake Thou wilt pardon and absolve all those who truly repent them of their sins. Grant us therefore true repentance, that we may be at peace with Thee, through the same Jesus Christ our Lord. Amen.

"O Lord, how manifold are thy works! In wisdom hast thou made them all. The earth is full of thy riches."—Ps. civ. 24.

O GOD, who as on this day of the week didst create great lights in the firmanent of the heaven, "the sun to rule the day, the moon and the stars to govern the night;" and who hast made them both for signs, and for seasons, whereby Thou refreshest and replenishest the earth; give us grace to thank Thee for these blessings, and to discern Thy glorious greatness in the glory of those things which Thou hast made. Make us to grow each

year in grace and heavenly wisdom, by the gift
of Thy Holy Spirit. Day by day let us magnify
Thee; remembering that the day and the night
are Thy work, marvellously designed for the
comfort and refreshment of Thy creatures. Make
us to spend our days in thy service. Make each
evening to remind us of the close of this life.
Let our nights be peaceable to us, as is the rest
of them that sleep in Jesus. Let each morning
be a token to us of our resurrection to eternal life
through Him. And year by year, as the time of
our departure draweth nigh, lead us to think more
and more of that "Sun of righteousness," "the
day spring from on high" who rose with healing in
his wings; even of Jesus our light and life, our
only Saviour and Redeemer. Amen.

Wednesday Evening.

"The Lord seeth not as man seeth; for man looketh on
the outward appearance, but the Lord looketh on the
heart."—1 Sam. xvi. 7.

O GOD, from whom no secrets are hidden,—who
knowest the hearts of men; and "understandest
their thoughts long before;" save us, we beseech
Thee, from the sin and folly of thinking to deceive
Thee. Make us to know the deceitfulness and
the deceivableness of our own hearts; and give
us grace to eschew hypocrisy; and whatsoever in

word or deed, would be false and insincere. Thou hast taught us by Thy Son Jesus Christ how hateful are the hypocrites in Thy sight—how terrible will be their condemnation. Thou hast taught us to love and seek, not the praise of men, but the praise of Thee our heavenly Father who seest in secret, and Thyself wilt reward us openly. Be merciful to us, and give us courage at all times to humble and abase ourselves before men, rather than that we win their praise, while our hearts are faithless and false to Thee. Let truth be our rule, and Thy favor the end of all our endeavours: that so we may approve ourselves in Thy sight, and be accepted of Thee as having indeed the spirit of Thy children, through Jesus Christ our Lord. Amen.

———

"Whatsoever ye do in word or deed, do all in the name of the Lord Jesus, giving thanks to God and the Father by him."—Col. iii. 17.

O GOD, whose "first and great commandment" to man is that we love Thee with all our hearts: who hast commanded us also by Thine apostle, saying, "in every thing give thanks," and whose blessed Son has also coupled together "the unthankful and the evil" as alike displeasing in Thy sight; give us grace, we beseech Thee, O heavenly Father, to love Thee, and to thank Thee for Thy great mercies, in all truth and sincerity of heart. Let not our professions of praise and thanksgiving issue out of feigned lips. Let not our hearts be far from Thee, when we draw nigh unto Thee with an appearance of devotion to give utterance to our prayers. But do Thou, of Thy great goodness, enable us to worship Thee, as Thou requirest, " in spirit and in truth ": ever loving Thee above all things—ever jealous for Thy glory and honour—ever mindful of Thy Presence and Thy Will: that so we may indeed be accounted Thine; and being cleansed by the blood of Thy dear Son, may be presented unto Thee without spot or blemish, by Him, and through Him, who with Thee and the Holy Spirit liveth and reigneth ever, one God, world without end. Amen.

Thursday Morning.

" If ye then be risen with Christ, seek those things which are above, where Christ sitteth on the right hand of God."—Col. iii. 1.

O LORD Jesus Christ, who hast ascended into heaven, and sittest at the right hand of God: look down upon us Thy servants, whom Thou hast redeemed. Lift up our hearts to Thee.— Make us by faith to see Thee where Thou art: and to set our affections on things above, desiring above all things so to live in this world that hereafter we may be partakers of Thy glory. Make us diligent to lay up our treasure in heaven, that so our hearts may be there also. And while we faithfully perform the duties Thou hast laid upon us in this life, encourage us daily to press toward the mark for the prize of our high calling of God in Thee. Thou hast said "if ye ask anything in My name, I will do it." Give us the desire to ask—to pray earnestly; and in our prayers to covet Thy best gifts—even the grace of Christian charity, and Thy Holy Comforter to abide within us. Enable us to believe that those whom Thou hast pronounced "blessed" are *blessed* indeed— the poor in spirit, the mourners, and the meek; they that hunger and thirst after righteousness; the merciful, the peacemakers, and the pure in heart. Give us grace that we may be numbered among these; and let our reward be great in heaven, through Thy mighty atonement and me- diation, O Jesus, who ever livest to make inter- cession for us. Amen.

"He that spared not his own Son, but delivered him up for us all, how shall he not with him also freely give us all things."—Rom viii. 32.

O GOD, who art slow to punish and mighty to save; long suffering, and of great goodness; we beseech Thee for the whole estate of Thy Church, that Thou wouldest replenish it with Thy spirit, and keep it evermore in Thy truth. We know,

O Lord, that Thou hast called us with Thine elect to exceeding great and precious promises. We know that Thou hast ordained unto salvation them whom Thou foreknewest—that Thou canst work in whom Thou wilt, faith, and obedience, and the abundant fruits of Thy Holy Spirit. But we believe also that Thou wilt not refuse any soul that loveth Thee. No man can call on Thee, but by Thy grace. "No man can say that Jesus is the Lord, but by the Holy Ghost." We believe therefore that in giving to us the hearty desire to pray unto Thee, and by inclining our hearts to believe in, and to seek Thy great salvation, Thou hast shown Thy goodwill towards us—that Thou givest not Thy grace in vain—that if Thou drawest us to Thy dear Son, He will in no wise cast us out. Accept us then, O heavenly Father, for His sake. Hear us, and help us, and sanctify us. And number us among Thine elect, through the same Thy Son Jesus Christ our Lord. Amen.

Thursday Evening.

"If ye know these things, happy are ye if ye do them."—John xiii. 17.

O LORD Jesus, who as on this day of the week, the evening Thou wast betrayed, didst teach Thy disciples many things that concerned their peace, who taughtest us humility by washing Thy servant's feet; and gavest us an example that we should do as Thou didst for them—who badest us love one another, as Thou hast loved us, that all men may know by this that we are Thy disciples—who didst declare that in Thy Father's house are many mansions—that Thou wast going to prepare a place for us, being Thyself "the way, the truth, and the life,"—give us grace, O Lord, humbly to receive and faithfully to follow Thy teaching. Give us grace to glorify Thy Father in Thee, by lifting up our earnest prayers to God in Thy name. Incline our hearts to obey Thy commandments in all things; and though Thou hast been taken from us, and received up into Thy glory, yet send to us that other Comforter who may continue with us, and comfort us for ever. Manifest Thyself to us by Him. Make us to love Thee and keep Thy words, that Thou and Thy heavenly Father may love us, and come unto us, and abide with us. Teach us all things, and bring us all things that Thou hast spoken to our remembrance, by the Holy Spirit. Make us to rejoice that Thou art gone to Thy Father; but leave Thy peace with us, even the peace of God which passeth all understanding, that it may keep our hearts and minds now and for evermore. Amen.

Thursday Evening.

"I am the true vine, and my Father is the husbandman."—John xv. 1.

O GOD, who by Thy Holy Spirit nurturest us, as Thou alone hast engrafted us, to be branches of the true vine Jesus our Lord, we beseech Thee to hear us, and to help us. Make us to be fruitful branches, that Thou take us not away : and purge us from all corrupt affections that daily we may bring forth more fruit. · Give us grace to abide in Him without whom we can do nothing. Give us grace to abound in good works that so Thou mayest be glorified. As Thou hast loved Thy dear Son, so hath He loved us. Enable us, by the keeping of His commandments, to continue in His love, that He may call us also His "friends." And above all make us mindful of His commandment given as on this night, "This do in remembrance of Me." Let the agonies of His death for us, and the shedding of His blood for our redemption be ever remembered thankfully by us all. And by constant obedience both to this, and to all His other sayings—by mortifying our carnal lusts, as well as by frequent receiving the blessed memorials of His sacrifice, and passion, enable us, in Thy mercy, to show the Lord's death till He come. Grant this, O heavenly Father, for the same Thy dear Son's sake. Amen.

Friday Morning.

"Let them say Spare thy people, O Lord, and give not ·
thine heritage to reproach."—Joel ii. 17.

O HOLY, Blessed, and Glorious Trinity, Three
Persons, and One God, have mercy upon us miserable sinners.

O Holy, Blessed and Glorious Trinity, &c.

Spare us, good Lord. Spare us Thy children, O
heavenly Father, and though we have grievously
sinned against Thee in thought, word, or deed;
yet for Thy dear Son's sake, and according to His
most gracious and forgiving prayer, Forgive us,
for we know not what we do. Lay not those sins
to our charge. Remember our infirmities. Call
to mind Thine own mercies of old time. Think
upon Thy holy covenant wherein Thou hast
promised to forgive our iniquity, and to remember our sins no more. Lord, we believe,
help Thou our unbelief. And let us claim to be
accounted children of Abraham Thy friend through
faith in Him whom Abraham by faith beheld afar
off, and believed. Take from us, we beseech
Thee, all hardness of heart, and contempt or neg-
lect of Thy word: and while we cling to Thy
precious promises of mercy and long suffering towards us as Thy children, make us diligent to love
and serve Thee, through Jesus Christ our Lord.
Amen.

" I pray not that thou shouldest take them out of the world but that thou shouldest keep them from the evil."—John xvii. 15.

DELIVER us, O heavenly Father, from all evil—from fornication and all uncleanness—from envy, hatred, and uncharitableness—from pride of heart, and rebellious thoughts against Thee. *Amen.*

Deliver us from worldliness, covetousness, and selfishness—from evil-speaking, lying, and slandering—from rejoicing either in iniquity, or in the afflictions and troubles of others. *Amen.*

Deliver us from strife, and contention—from false doctrine, and schism—from unthankfulness to Thee, or to our neighbours who have dealt kindly with us—from forgetfulness of our duty to all men as Thy creatures—to all Christians as specially Thy *children,* and brethren with ourselves of Christ. *Amen.*

Hear us, O God, in all our troubles and adversities; nor leave us in the days of our youth and health, our prosperity and success. Leave us not to ourselves when our own hearts would endanger us. Forsake us not when we are surrounded by dangers and temptations from without. But ever watch over us, and defend us, and mightily deliver us; strengthening and comforting our hearts, that we may both serve and trust in Thee, through Jesus Christ Thy Son our Saviour and Redeemer. Amen.

———

" Pray for them which despitefully use you, and persecute you."—Mat. v. 44.

O LORD, who hast taught us not only to pray for ourselves, but to intercede for others—for our enemies, as well as for our friends; we beseech Thee for all who are in danger or trouble. Be merciful to them. Forgive their sins. Defend them, and give them seasonable relief from all their afflictions. Bring back the erring to Thy way, and to the knowledge of Thy truth; and extend Thy saving health unto all men. Hear us, O Jesus, who prayedst for Thy murderers; and hast taught us to forgive, as we hope to be forgiven. Hear us, and give to us and to all men true repentance and faith in Thee our blessed Lord and Saviour. Amen.

———

Friday Evening.

"Thou sayest I am rich and increased with goods, and have need of nothing; and knowest not that thou art wretched, and miserable, and poor, and blind, and naked."—Rev. iii. 17.

O GOD, who, in Thy tender love to man, deliveredst up Thy Son Jesus Christ, to be (as on this day of the week,) slain for us upon the cross, a sacrifice for our sins; and to shed His precious blood, that Thy Covenant for our salvation might be perfected; Grant, we beseech Thee, that to us the benefits of His death and bloodshedding may be made sure. Give us faith to lay hold of the blessings which by that great Sacrifice He hath purchased for us. Give us grace to look upon Him who was pierced—to think of Him as He hung upon the tree, "bearing our sins in His own body,"—nailing to the cross and cancelling the law of Ordinances which was against us; and procuring for us His enemies "the spirit of grace and of supplications." Give us, O heavenly Father, abundantly of that spirit. Incline our hearts to pray. Make us to know our great necessities—that before Thee we are "poor, and blind, and naked." And do Thou, O heavenly Father, hear us, and help us—giving us the true riches of Thy spirit—opening the eyes of our understanding that we know may Thee—and clothing us with the righteousness, of Thy dear Son—for His sake, Jesus Christ our Lord. Amen.

"Reckon ye also yourselves to be dead indeed unto sin; but alive unto God through Jesus Christ our Lord." Rom. vi. 11.

LORD Jesus, who, after the suffering of death for us, wast, as on this night, laid to rest in Thy grave—to keep there that sabbath which was indeed ordained for us men—for our redemption and salvation—hear us, good Lord, and have mercy upon us, that as Thou didst rest in the sleep of death, so we may also hereafter find *rest*, and be raised again unto eternal life through Thee. Grant us grace to keep our sabbath henceforth in the laying aside of all works of ungodliness and sin. Let us rest—yea, let us die, unto sin: and live again unto righteousness, and to Thy service. Quicken us also by the Holy Spirit which is in Thee, as Thou hast power to quicken whom Thou wilt. Quicken us in this world unto every good work. And, as we believe in Thee, so let us have everlasting life, and raise us up at the last day. Grant this, O merciful Jesus, our Lord, and only Saviour. Amen.

"In that he himself hath suffered being tempted, he is able to succour them that are tempted."—Heb. ii. 18.

WE beseech Thee, O Lord Jesus, by Thine agony and bloody sweat, by Thy cross and suffering, by Thy precious death and burial, by Thy glorious resurrection and ascension, and by the coming of the Holy Ghost, good Lord deliver us from all dangers. Save us and help us, as we do put our trust in Thee. Let us not fall from Thee. Let us not deny Thee. If our faith is weak, pray for us that it fail not. If our danger is great, succour us. Strengthen, and encourage, and mightily deliver us, O Captain of our salvation, for Thy mercy's sake. Amen.

Saturday Morning.

" Let us labour therefore to enter into that Rest, lest any man fall after the same example of unbelief."—Heb. iv. 11.

O GOD, creator of all things, who, as on this the seventh day of the week, didst rest from all Thy work. Who by Thy prophet David didst speak also yet again of a "rest" whereinto some must enter—even the rest that "remaineth to the people of God"; grant that we may attain unto this rest, as well as keep Thy true sabbath here on earth, by abstaining from every evil work, and seeking peace unto our souls. Make us to think this day of Jesus Thy dear Son, as in the rest and stillness of the grave. Give us grace, that as He died unto sin once, and was at rest; so we may now be dead indeed unto sin—free from sin, as they are that be dead—but alive by the spirit unto God, to serve Thee in righteousness—to worship Thee in spirit and in truth. We beseech Thee, O God, both to accept our service, and to pardon our offences. Be merciful to us miserable offenders. Though we be unprofitable as servants, yet let us be dear to Thee as Thy children. Be Thou our king, and we Thy people—safe under the defence of Thy right hand. Bless the labours of Thy servants both to our comfort, and for Thy glory. Grant us health, and happiness in this world, so far as Thou seest to be good for us. And in the world to come bring us to everlasting life through Jesus Christ our Lord. Amen.

"Provide yourselves bags which wax not old, a treasure in the heavens that faileth not."—Luke xii. 33.

O LORD Jesus, our master and heavenly teacher, who hast commended works of mercy done as on this day; and shown us that the sabbath being made for man, whatever is for the true comfort and well-being of man, may then lawfully be done; give us grace to lay Thy words to heart, and throughout our christian sabbath to be diligent in doing good. Not on the seventh day only, but every day; thereby showing that to refrain from evil is our "rest," and to be doing the works of Him who has revealed Himself as a merciful God. In this our last day of bodily [or worldly] labour, make us to think, not of our gains only for this life, but of the treasure we are laying up in heaven by acts of kindness, liberality, and love. And let our care be also to seek acceptance of these by Thee through faith, not in our own merits, or in the value of our good deeds, but in Thy mercy, and in the merits of Jesus

Christ Thy Son, for whose sake alone, and through whom we beseech Thee to accept our service and our prayers. Amen.

Saturday Evening.

"Covet earnestly the best gifts."—1 Cor. xii. 31.

ALMIGHTY God, maker of all things, judge of all men, merciful to hear our prayers, and mighty to save; hear us, we beseech Thee, as Thou hast promised by Thy dear Son, when we ask in His name. Incline our hearts to pray according to Thy will. Teach us, O God, to know our greatest needs—to ask Thy best gifts—to value what Thou who lovest us, wouldest give us for our good. Give us an understanding heart, and ready will to follow the guidance of Thy Holy Spirit. Give us a desire for heavenly things, that we may hunger and thirst after righteousness. Give us an abhorrence and loathing for what is sinful, impure, and hateful in Thy sight. Make us zealous for Thine honour, yet with gentleness and charity towards all men. Make us to glorify Thee by good works—by our patience and humility, and the manifestation of a spirit from above. But above all, be merciful to our sins. Daily we have offended Thee in will, word, or deed. Daily do Thou forgive whatever we have done amiss,

for Thy dear Son's sake Jesus Christ our Lord.
Amen.

"If by any means I might attain unto the resurrection of
the dead."—Phil. iii. 11.

O HEAVENLY Father, who hast placed us
amidst the dangers and temptations of this
troublesome world, that Thou mightest humble
us, and prove us, to do us good at our latter end;
who hast made this life our time of trial—eternal
glory our great reward if we do well—eternal
misery our condemnation if we do evil: in Thy
mercy incline our hearts to weigh well these
solemn truths, that we waste not precious time—
that we think not this world our home—that we
forget not the end of our pilgrimage—that "city
which hath its foundations, whose Builder and
Maker is God." Lord, stir up in us a longing to
reach safely, in Thine own good time, the end of
our Christian course. Let no worldly cares or
pleasures efface that glorious prize from our
thoughts. And grant that we neither weary in
our efforts to attain it, nor slack our going forward,
nor turn aside from the narrow path which leadeth
unto life eternal. But do Thou help us onward,
as Thou hast brought us to Thy way. Lift us
up when we are fallen. Cheer us and encourage

us when the hindrances to our progress are great. And finally bring us to the inheritance of Thy saints, through Jesus Christ our Saviour. Amen.

A Prayer to be added when the Holy Communion has been received.

" We being many are one bread and one body, for we are all partakers of that one bread."—1 Cor. x. 17.

O MERCIFUL Saviour, who hast nourished our souls this day with the sacrament of Thy Body and Blood: giving us faith to feed on the hope of everlasting life through the Sacrifice of Thy Body, and through the "New Covenant" in Thy most precious Blood—who hast assured us, by the holy pledges of bread and wine received according to Thy word, that we are very members incorporate of Thy mystical Body, the Church: and included in the "Everlasting Covenant" wherein alone we can have pardon, and peace, and life; hear us, we beseech Thee, and confirm us in that faith. Knit our hearts, by the bonds of love and charity, to all those who have like blessed fellowship in Thee with ourselves. Make us mindful of the mercies, and spiritual privileges we have received, and so dwell in us by Thy Holy Spirit, that we may be a holy temple "meet for the Master's use," and worthy of Thy presence, O Lord our Saviour and Redeemer. Amen.

*To be used when the Holy Sacrament of Baptism
has been administered.*

"Take heed that ye despise not one of these little ones ;
for I say unto you that in heaven their angels do
always behold the face of my Father which is in heaven."—Mat. xviii. 10.

O JESUS, who in our congregation of Thy church
hast received this day a new member of Thy mystical Body—admitting *him* to Thy holy baptism—
washing away *his* sins—sanctifying *him* unto
God—and making *him*, as Thou hast once made us,
* one of Thy Father's children, and heir of Thy
kingdom of heaven, give us grace to welcome
among us this new *brother*, and to rejoice for *him*
in that Thou hast saved *his* soul from the condemnation of the world.   Make us to seek *his*
continuance in Thy salvation, to help *him* forward
in *his* Christian warfare by good example, by
wholesome precept, and by earnest prayer.   And
meanwhile make us to regard *him* as now a
brother through Thee, and precious to us, because
precious in Thy sight.   Keep *him*, O Lord, and
keep us evermore in Thy faith and fear, that we
may continue Thine for ever, and be brought to
the full fruition of eternal life, through Thee our
only Lord and Saviour.   Amen.

---

* N.B.—When the plural pronoun is used, for "*one*"
read "*of the number.*"

A Prayer to be used in time of apprehended Trial or Affliction.

"Call upon me in the day of trouble: I will deliver thee, and thou shall glorify me."—Ps. l. 15.

O ALMIGHTY God, maker and preserver of all things, our heavenly Father, who lovest all that Thou hast made, and specially those whom Thou hast adopted to be Thine own children through Thy Son Jesus Christ; we beseech Thee, O heavenly Father, at this time hear our prayer, which in our fear of severe trial and affliction we would lift up to Thee. We beseech Thee, Comfort us and calm our fears. Without Thee, O God, "not a sparrow falleth on the ground." In Thy sight "the very hairs of our head are all numbered." Thou knowest then our thoughts, and the sorrow of our hearts. Make us to know and feel that affliction cometh not by chance, but from Thy hand; not in anger, but in love; not needlessly, but in Thy wisdom and mercy for our good, for good to all that love Thee, whether Thou wilt that they abide longer here, or "depart and be with Christ which is far better." Make us to perceive in this and all our troubles, that which we ought to do; and having done that, to put our trust in Thee. If it be Thy gracious pleasure to deliver us from the sorrow which hangeth over us, make us thankful, humbly thankful, and give

us grace to set forth Thy praise not in word only
but in deed, not with our lips only but in our
lives. Or if it be Thy will that what we fear
should come to pass, that trouble should overtake
us, and that great affliction should try our faith
and chasten us, "Thy will O God be done."
"It is the Lord, let Him do what seemeth Him
good." Teach us to submit ourselves wholly to
Thy will, and so to make affliction profitable to
us. And let this be our comfort that Thou
knowest what is best for us, Thou canst make all
things work together for good to them that love
Thee. Sorrow may endure for a night, but joy
cometh in the morning. Let us think that Thou
our Father wilt have joy for us when the night
of death is past, and the glorious day of everlasting life shall dawn upon Thy saints, through
Jesus Christ our Lord. Amen.

Daily Praise

N. B.—The Evening Anthems if not used in the evening may serve for the mornings of alternate weeks.

Sunday Morning.

O Lord, open Thou our lips.

And our mouth shall show forth Thy praise.

1   To Him who hath loved us, and sought us out when we were lost : and hath taken us for His children, that we may love and rejoice in Him.—

2   Be all praise and thanksgiving now and for evermore.   Amen.

3   To Him who hath died for us, bearing our sins in His own body; and hath purchased our pardon, and an inheritance for us of everlasting glory.—

4   Be glory, and thanksgiving, might, victory, and dominion, for ever and ever.   Amen.

5   To Him who sanctifieth and quickeneth the soul of man—Lord and giver of life.— |

6   Be worship and adoration, thanksgiving and praise, throughout all ages for ever.   Amen.

Glory be to the Father, and to the Son : and to the Holy Ghost ;

As it was in the beginning, is now, and ever shall be : world without end. Amen.

Sunday Evening.

Lord show Thy servants Thy work, and we will praise Thee.

Show Thy children Thy glory, and we will magnify Thee.

1   Let us praise Him that made us, let us thank Him for His infinite mercies.

2   For our safety under the defence of His right hand—for His Fatherly love towards us.

3   O God that wouldest have no soul perish, but that all should turn unto Thee and be saved :

4   Receive us when we come unto Thee : turn us that we seek Thee earnestly.

5   Blessed be He that hath given us hope of mercy. Blessed be the good shepherd who seeketh his lost sheep.

6   Blessed be He that healeth the broken hearted. Blessed be He that converteth sinners unto Himself.

Monday Morning.

O Lord, open Thou our lips.

And our mouth shall show forth Thy praise.

1   Let us praise the name of God with thanksgiving : let us tell of all His marvellous works.

2 We whom He hath taken to be His children: let us love Him as our Father, and glorify Him by obedience to His will.

3 O God Thou hast called us to Thy salvation, Thou hast sent us a mighty deliverer, even Jesus Christ Thy Son.

4 Thou sparedst not Thine only begotten for our redemption. Thou deliveredst Him up to death for our sakes.

5 Thou gavest Him power of life: and to give life unto us.

6 That we through Him might live for evermore.

Monday Evening.

Lord show Thy servants Thy work, and we will praise Thee.

Show Thy children Thy glory, and we will magnify Thee.

1 For the incarnation of Thy eternal Son and Word—that He came down from heaven for us men, and was made man.—

2 All thanks, and praise, and glory, be unto Thee, O Father Almighty. Amen.

3 For Thy death and passion, O Lamb of God slain for our sins.—

4 Be all praise and thanksgiving unto Thee, from us miserable sinners, whom Thou diedst to save. Amen.

5 For that Thou, O righteous Father, hast accepted the sacrifice; and raised up Thy Son Jesus Christ for our justification.—

6 We thank, and praise, and magnify Thy holy name. Blessing and glory be unto Thee, O God, now and for ever. Amen.

Tuesday Morning.

O Lord, open Thou our lips.
And our mouth shall show forth Thy praise.

1 Let us magnify the love of our Redeemer, and call to mind His mercies towards us.

2 Let us remember the everlasting covenant given unto Him of the Father, that He might overcome sin and death, and save us from destruction.

3 By Thy blood of the Covenant Thou hast cleansed us, O Christ; by Thy death, O Lamb of God, Thou hast taken away our sins.

4 When Thou hadst overcome the sharpness of death, Thou didst open the kingdom of heaven to all believers.

5 Thou art exalted to be a Prince, and a Saviour, to give deliverance to Thy people.

6 We therefore praise Thee, our Lord and King, for ever and ever.

Tuesday Evening.

Lord show Thy servants Thy work, and we will praise Thee.

Show Thy children Thy glory, and we will magnify Thee.

1 Let us praise Him who hath overcome death; and opened unto us the gate of everlasting life.

2 Let us glorify Him whose soul was not left in Hell; neither His flesh did see corruption.

3 Blessed be He who delivereth us from the power of death : who giveth us the victory through Jesus Christ our Lord.

4 And blessed be He who hath taken away the victory from the grave : and hath taken from death his sting.

5 The sting of death is sin. Give us grace, O Jesus, to overcome sin.

5 And quicken us by Thy Holy Spirit unto everlasting life through Thee.

Wednesday Morning.

O Lord, open Thou our lips.

And our mouth shall show forth Thy praise.

1 We believe in Thee, O God the Father; that Thou hast made all things; and lovest us; and hast sent Thy Son to save us.

Answer. *Amen.*

2   We believe in Thee, Lord Jesus Christ: that Thou art Son of God, and Son of Man: everlasting: and hast died for our sins, and risen again for our justification.

Answer. *Amen.*

3   We believe in Thee, O Holy Spirit; that Thou sanctifiest us; and governest the hearts of the righteous; and alone canst quicken us unto life eternal.

Answer. *Amen.*

Glory be to the Holy Trinity, Three Persons, but One God.

Answer.   Glory be to the Father, &c.

As it was in the beginning, &c.

Wednesday Evening.

Lord show Thy servants Thy work, and we will praise Thee.

Show Thy children Thy glory, and we will magnify Thee.

1   We praise Thee, O God; that Thou hast raised up a *Son of Man* from death; that Thou hast set Him on the throne of Thy glory.

2   We thank Thee that Thou hast given unto Him dominion—even a kingdom which ruleth over all.

3   Where He is, there, He has said, shall his servants be: we shall be made like unto Him:

we shall reign with Him, and see Him as He is.

4 Lord God, for this promise be thanks and praise unto Thee. For this most glorious hope make us to love and serve Thee.

5 Keep us in Thy way, O Lord, that we slip not.

6 Leave us not, nor forsake us, O God of our salvation.

Thursday Morning.

O Lord, open Thou our lips.

And our mouth shall show forth Thy praise.

1 Let us praise Him who moved upon the face of the waters, to give life. Let us worship Him who giveth life in the hearts of men.

2 O Holy Ghost the Comforter, let us rejoice unto Thee with reverence. Rule Thou, O Holy Spirit, in our hearts.

3 Dwell within us, and forsake us not; guide our steps, and be a light unto our paths.

4 Strengthen the feeble soul, and work mightily in our hearts: vanquish the spirit of evil in us, and destroy it utterly.

5 We pray Thee, O God, help us that we grieve Thee not. Keep us ever, that we sin not against Thee.

E

6 And the glorious majesty of the Lord our God be upon us, like as we do put our trust in Thee.

Thursday Evening.

Lord, show Thy servants Thy work, and we will praise Thee.

Show Thy children Thy glory, and we will magnify Thee.

1 Jesus, Thou hast ascended up on high; Thou hast led captivity captive.

2 Thou sittest at the right hand of God; Thou ever livest to make intercession for us.

3 Thou hast entered into the tabernacle of the heavens. With Thine own blood Thou hast presented Thyself before the mercy seat of the Almighty.

4 Thou offerest there the acceptable sacrifice. Thou art our priest and advocate with the Father.

5 Through Thee have we access to the holiest. Through Thee may we draw nigh unto the God of Heaven.

6 Thanks be to Thee who hast been touched with the feeling of our infirmities; and art a merciful and faithful High Priest to make reconciliation for Thy people.

Friday Morning.

O Lord, open Thou our lips.

And our mouth shall show forth Thy praise.

1 While we live will we praise the Lord: and bless His name for ever and ever.

2 The Lord is gracious and longsuffering: our God is full of compassion, and of great goodness.

3 It is the Lord that preserveth us, and keepeth us alive. It is our heavenly Father that feedeth us from day to day.

4 It is our God that hath saved us from the condemnation of death eternal. It is He that hath found an atonement for us that our sins might be blotted out.

5 It is the Lord that pleadeth for us before the throne of mercy. It is our God who is for us; and who then shall be against us?

6 It is He, our Redeemer, that sendeth unto us His holy Comforter. Let us be strong in His salvation: and praise His name for ever.

Friday Evening.

Lord, show Thy servants Thy work, and we will praise Thee.

Show Thy children Thy glory, and we will magnify Thee.

1 Thou to whom all judgment is committed, who shall not honour Thee? Thou who art judge of quick and dead, who shall not fear Thy name?

2 The hour cometh when all that are in the grave shall hear Thy voice : when every eye shall see Thee, and shall look on Him whom they pierced.

3 We therefore pray Thee, help Thy servants whom Thou hast redeemed with Thy precious blood.

4 Make us to be numbered with Thy saints, that Thou enter not into judgment with us, but receive us into Thy glory.

5 O Lord, have mercy upon us; have mercy upon us.

6 Lord, let Thy mercy lighten upon us, as we do put our trust in Thee.

Saturday Morning.

O Lord, open Thou our lips.
And our mouth shall show forth Thy praise.

1 Great and marvellous are Thy works, Lord God Almighty; just and true are Thy ways, Thou king of saints.

2 Thou hast founded Thy church upon a rock, and it abideth: even upon Thyself the rock of ages, whose goings forth have been from everlasting.

3 Thou visitest Thy saints, and refreshest them with Thy presence. Thou, O Christ, art with us, even unto the end of the world.

4 Thou canst cleanse the defiled heart. By Thy spirit Thou canst turn sinners unto God.

5 Mighty art Thou, O God our Saviour. Turn us and deliver us that we may find our life in Thee.

6 And give us faith in Thee that we may be children of Thy Father; and renew us daily in the spirit of our God.

Saturday Evening.

Lord, show Thy servants Thy work, and we will praise Thee.

Show Thy children Thy glory, and we will magnify Thee.

1 O Lord God, there is mercy with Thee, therefore shalt Thou be feared.

2 To the Lord our God belong mercies and forgivenesses: therefore let us return unto Him.

3 Thou willest not the death of sinner. Thou wouldest have all men come to the knowledge of Thy truth.

4 Thou hast shown us Thy salvation, Thou hast brought us into the way of life.

5 Great is the peace which Thou hast prepared for us, and the glory Thou wouldest give us.

·6 We therefore praise Thee for Thy loving-kindness towards us, and will magnify Thee, O Lord, in the congregation of Thy saints.

INDEX TO FAMILY PRAYERS.